Itchybald Scratchet

Blown Away!

by

Sue C. Medcalf

Published

by

Bishops Lydeard – Somerset – UK

ISBN 978 0 9955395 2 5

9 780995 539525

Itchybald Scratchet

Blown Away!

Copyright © Sue C. Medcalf

Published by SCM Books July 2018
Cover design SCM Books
Illustrations: Nicole Poulsom
Editor: Proof Professor

*   *   *   *   *   *

Sue C Medcalf

About the Author

Sue C. Medcalf

Born in Bedford, Sue's passion has been her family with no thoughts of writing.

Having finally put pen to paper, finding the experience rewarding and therapeutic, Sue is now involved in an ongoing writing project, capitalising on her interest and research into badgers and wildlife in general, along with their behaviour and habitat. Her intention is to encourage children of all ages to benefit, enjoy and learn from reading.

Her family moved from Bedford to Somerset in the 1990's, thereby enriching her understanding and enjoyment of nature and the countryside. The conflict between the need for human development owing to the increase in population and wildlife has been motivational to her writing.

Find out more at www.itchybaldscratchet.co.uk or e-mail to sales@itchybaldscratchet.co.uk

About the Illustrator

Nicole Poulsom

Born and raised in Durban, South Africa, the eldest of two, Nicole was raised in an animal-friendly home and always had some form of pet. They were usually cats or a dog, but have also included rats, mice, fish and the odd budgie. She even helped catch snakes for her younger brother's collection. Nicole loved drawing and painting from a young age, but lacked the confidence to use her talents until now.

Now living in the UK, Nicole is happily settled in Kent with her husband, cat and spaniel, who all emigrated from South Africa. Having developed a passion for British wildlife, she is delighted to be included in this amazing project about Itchybald Scratchet and his friends.

"It is a wonderful thought that people reading this series will enjoy the characters created by the author. I hope my interpretation of Itchy and his friends enhances the story and enjoyment when reading about their adventures."

*   *   *   *   *   *   *

DEDICATION

This publication is dedicated to my Grandson Kyle Medcalf, (1997-2016).

The inspiration for writing is from my sister, Dawn, without whom the *Itchybald Scratchet* series wouldn't have started. After all, would you know what to do if you found badgers at the bottom of your garden? I did some research on badgers and their way of life, which lead me to write the book. My sister and I share a similar humour and our badger conversations developed into an amusing story, resulting in these publications.

I would particularly like to thank Nicole for producing all the sketches used in the story. Thanks also to Matt (Proof Professor) for his valuable help and advice in helping with editing.

The project continues to grow and none of this would have been possible without the help and support of my husband, Ian, my supportive family Alan, Denise, Scott and Dawn, friends and neighbours, to whom I am truly indebted. They have encouraged me to carry on with the series during difficult times experienced by most writers!

*   *   *   *   *   *   *

Characters in Blown Away!

Badger   Itchybald Scratchet (Itchy)

Mouse   Enormouse (Norm)

Wombat   Wanda

Spinifex Mouse   Squeaky

Mountain Lion   Roamin

Groundhogs   Repeater
                      Ditto
                      Chuck

People   Upples

Itchy's journey so far...

The Tales Begin - Badger Wood is under threat from Upples (People) who want to build houses on their home. Itchybald Scratchet (Itchy) to his friends is distracted by news of Upples building and has a fall, but he is rescued by Enormouse (Norm) who becomes Itchy's best friend.

Rainbow Ravine - Itchy and his friends find gold to put in the ground to deter the Upples from building. If it is a historical site it will be saved, but Silky, an albino badger saves their home as she is so different. Later, when an Upple man discovers a gold coin, their home is threatened once again.

The Missing Friend - One of the characters goes missing leading to a further adventure for Itchy, who is the missing character and do they find him? There is more contact with the Upples Itchy is trying to avoid.

The Heat Is On – Itchy receives a map from Auntie Twiddle and embarks on a dangerous journey and finds himself in Australia. Norm is also in Australia but somehow appears in a different place. The two friends are reunited and Itchy realises after listening to an Aboriginal song they travelled at the wrong time.

Stropple To The Rescue –Stropple the camel and other wildlife come to Itchy's rescue in this latest adventure. Norm as always, is hungry for his favourite pizza and gets into more trouble! Itchy and his friends think they know the way back home but then get caught in a forest fire. As they are running away from the flames Itchy thinks he can hear Fidget calling him. Is it Fidget?

Find out in book 6 Blown Away!

Blown Away!

Stropple the camel is Itchy's Australian friend. His thick fur is now burnt, and almost black around his knobbly knees as he calls out in alarm to Itchy.

"You can't go back into the fire! Run! Itchy, run! It's just the noise of the flames, no one can survive, run, run!" he urged desperately, panting for every breath, his lungs felt as if they would burst at any moment.

Just for an instant, Itchy hesitated. He looked at Stropple's distraught face and then towards Norm who was a few Upple heights in front of him. Poor Norm, Itchy could see he was covered in a fine, grey dust, and bits of crisp leafy debris and twigs stuck to his once shiny mouse coat. His whiskers were curly and singed, he looked a sorry sight.

"Is it Fidgets voice?" Itchy asked the frightened creature reluctantly, not wanting to hear the answer.

"I'm afraid I think it is," answered Norm, trembling, his voice shaking as he tried to stop his knees knocking together.

"I will come with you to find him" he said bravely, braver than he felt, although the quiver in his voice gave him away. He couldn't let Itchy go in on his own even if he was afraid.

"No, I won't hear of it!" Itchy declared, determined not to risk the life of his friend. He lifted up his paw, and quickly scratching at his leg he shouted,

"Go with Stropple, I won't be long and we will catch you up. He can't be far behind or we wouldn't have heard him calling out to us."

Branches and brittle twigs snapped beneath Itchy's paws as he ran clumsily across the scorched earth, the other animals went hurrying past him in the opposite direction in pursuit of safety.

"Itchy!" the voice called out, weaker and hoarser now, then almost a whisper. "Itchy, is that you?"

On hearing this voice again, Itchy was in no doubt it was Fidget, and bravely turned and ran back towards the clouds of dense smoke. His black and white coat didn't offer much protection against the searing heat. But it was the dusty ash which affected Itchy the most. He stumbled towards Fidget's call, trying to cover his badger's nose with his paw. His eyes were streaming and half-closed as he struggled to see where he was going. Itchy had to listen hard, as he tried to make his way towards the now fragile call of his friend.

"Itchy! Oh Itchy! How glad I am to see you!" Dull, grey and almost completely covered in soft ash, there lay Fidget on the scorched earth. He kept trying to lift his head up from his front paws, he had used all his strength to call out for help. Itchy scratched at his brow: he had no idea how they were going to escape the flames now.

How would he manage to help Fidget on his own?

"Come on," he said determinedly as he put out his singed paws to help his wounded badger friend to his feet.

"You can't stay here: try to stand up so I can help you. How on Badger's earth did you get here anyway? I thought you were back in Badger Wood with the others!"

"I followed you and Norm through the doorway," whispered Fidget quietly. He tried to sit up but every inch of him ached with the effort. Itchy could barely hear his voice, it was so hoarse due to the smoke and he wondered if Fidget would ever be able to speak properly or whistle happily again. He had to lean in close to hear what his friend was saying.

Fidget continued, his voice rasping quietly as his throat was very sore.

"I only hesitated for a badger's moment and then I followed you and Norm through the old door. I have wandered about for ages in this strange land, searching in burrows and hiding from Upples to try and find a way home. Then this fire started, and I heard you and Norm calling to each other." He smiled weakly at Itchy, the relief showing on his dirty brow as he tried to smile at his brave friend.

The two badgers clung tightly together through the thick, grey smoke as they tried to find their way out. They stumbled together over the burnt ground, trying to avoid the hottest parts of the glowing dirt around them.

Ash floated on the wind, like small pieces of grey snow, giving a surreal, unnatural appearance to their surroundings. They seemed to walk a very long way, and Itchy's back paw was now very sore, as it was bearing Fidget's weight as well as his own.

Itchy helps Fidget walk, limping to safety

Every time he walked a long way or carried a lot of weight, Itchy's paw ached: since his fall down the well in Badger Wood it had never been the same.

Fidget leaned heavily against Itchy's side, whose arm and back also ached now with the weight of the wounded badger. Just as they thought they would both collapse, Norm appeared coughing and spluttering. Itchy had never been so glad to see his large mouse friend. Norm's whiskers were covered in small globules of grey spittle and the edges of his coat were singed. Bravely ignoring his fear of fire, he was making his way slowly through the smoke to rescue his friends! He held his large, red hanky to his nose, his eyes streaming as he appeared in front of them.

"Grab hold of my tail!" said Norm determinedly as he turned and whisked his very long tail onto the ground. He stepped quickly from one foot to the other, trying to ignore the heat emanating from the red-hot ashes, towards his friends.

"It will never drag both of us!" said Itchy, coughing loudly as he tried to clear his throat, concern for his brave mouse friend in his voice.

"Yes it will," said Norm. "My tail is very strong, if you remember? And anyway, we can't be far from safety now."

So the big mouse with his very long tail once again had come to their rescue. His body bent over from the weight of his two friends, he dragged and pulled the injured badgers slowly along through the charred remains of the bush until they were clear of the searing heat.

****

After the fire

Eventually they came to a small clearing; somehow they had escaped the fire. Surrounded by scrub-land and rock it felt safe, but where on Badger's earth were they? There was no sign of Stropple or of Wanda. No sign of anyone else at all.

As the air cleared the three friends slept soundly, exhausted; only the smell of smoke which still clung to the badger's fur gave any clue of the danger they had been in. On waking, his fur all tangled and messy, his white markings dull and greyish in colour, Itchy scratched madly. Fidget, true to his name, couldn't get comfortable at all. He wriggled around whilst grooming, muttering under his breath and trying to clear his throat which was very sore. He tried to speak but was unable to; his tongue was dry and cracked. Fidget gave out a harsh, hacking, bark-like cough every time he opened his mouth to speak.

Norm, still tired out, lay flat on his back gazing at the night sky, wondering once more how he had got himself into this mess. Oh to be back in Badger Wood! Preferably sitting by the fire with a nice big slice of cheese and tomato pizza! Even the thought of Matty's worm stew, thick, slippery and juicy, conjured up warm, pleasant feelings of home.

Thinking of pizza and food in general was making Norm hungry and his belly rumbled noisily in protest. He stood up to take in their surroundings, and see if there was anything at all to eat. But all he could see was the usual dry, scrubby dirt, nothing edible at all.

"Where are we?" he asked the others rubbing at his red sore eyes, trying to ignore the noise of his hungry belly growling loudly, as he looked around him.

"I don't know," Itchy replied still scratching, "but the earth is the same colour so we must still be in Australia."

He looked over at poor Fidget; he was still coughing and trying to clear his throat. A tiny whisper was all he could manage. Much to his dismay, try as he might, Fidget still couldn't whistle either. He lay exhausted, his back propped against a sheer rock-face his, chin resting on his chest, and his eyes downcast and sad.

Fidget tries to whistle

Looking around him, Itchy could see a high, sheer cliff rising up in front of him: a craggy gorge seemed to have been carved into the earth somehow and it was so high he couldn't see the top of it.

There was a scurrying sound nearby; curious as to what the noise was Itchy went over to a sandy mound to investigate. A small, brown mouse leapt into the air right under Itchy's nose, which made him jump. It squeaked in surprise: she too hadn't expected to see anyone.

"Hi, I'm Squeaky," she said smiling at Itchy, her long whiskers twitching wildly. She seemed very friendly.

"I'm a Spinifex mouse," she announced proudly standing upright on her little hind legs while using her tail for balance as she cleaned her whiskers.

"The Upples call us Hoppies because we hop about."

"Where are we?" Itchy asked her while scratching at his ears dislodging bits of burnt twig. Looking around him, he knew they were lost. But at least there seemed to be some large green trees for shade not too far away. Also, there were shrubs near them this time so hopefully some nice fat juicy worms for supper. Seeing the mouse eating was making Itchy hungry, he couldn't remember the last time he had eaten.

Squeaky continued:

"This area is a nature reserve called Kata Tjuta and you are in Kings Canyon which has walks for Upples. Uluru is near here. My family and I live nearby and we eat the crumbs that the Upples leave behind from their lunches." The mouse was still licking her whiskers clean and wiping her paws together delicately as she spoke.

"Where are you from?" she asked, carefully cleaning up every last morsel with her tiny paws so she didn't miss anything. "I've never seen you round here before."

Itchy introduced Fidget and Norm to the mouse; she couldn't seem to stay still for very long and kept hopping up into the air, much to Itchy's amusement. It was all he could do to stop himself from laughing at this small creature's antics. He couldn't help but laugh as he tried to explain to the mouse all about their journey and how they were saving Badger Wood from being built on. It was difficult when she kept doing somersaults; his words tumbled out as he spoke quickly.

"But now...." continued Itchy, moving his head up and down in a bobbing motion as he watched the mouse frantically jumping.

"Fidget's lost his voice due to the bush fire so he can only whisper and he's lost his whistle too. Can you think of anything to mend his throat and for us to find our way home? Is there any water nearby? I heard an Upple singing about Uluru having caves: if we go there will we be able to find our back to Badger Wood? "

Squeaky a Spinifex mouse

"Ok ok, slow down!" Squeaky replied smiling, not used to such a barrage of questions from a badger.

"There is a waterhole called the Garden of Eden near here: a drink of water might help your friend Fidget to get his voice back, I expect he's thirsty. Then I can show you the way to Uluru. Follow me."

She hopped off at such an amazing speed across the red, dusty soil that the three friends struggled to keep up. Norm was the first to catch up with her; he couldn't get over the difference in size!

"You are sooo small!" Norm said, grinning broadly as he caught up with his new tiny friend and ran alongside her.

"And you are so big for a mouse!" Squeaky replied. "Why are you sooo big?"

Norm puffed as he tried to keep up; he still hadn't recovered from the effects of breathing in the smoke. He was getting used to other animals' reactions to his size by now and replied:

"I got stuck in a pizza factory when I was small; I ate too much and couldn't get out of the hole I had used to get in. Then I just ate more and more and I grew and grew into an enormous mouse! Cheese and tomato pizza is my favourite food now! I would rather eat that than anything else!" Although, Norm was quick to add, "I love all Upple food!"

"Oooh! Sometimes there are pieces of pizza left here," said Squeaky helpfully. She looked up at Norm who was smiling broadly at the mention of Upple food; he really was very, very large for a mouse, she thought to herself.

"The Upples throw food away when they are full up; if you keep looking at the ground you might be lucky enough to find some!"

Squeaky somersaulted backwards happily, with her long tail flipping around her, Norm laughed with her, making sure he kept one eye on the ground just in case this small mouse happened to be right and there might just be pizza about.

Fidget looked at Itchy and whispered as loud as he could to his friend:

"I hope he finds some pizza soon: Norm has been miserable without his favourite food." Fidget coughed harshly; the hacking sound even sounded quiet against the cicadas' noise which was ever-present in the background.

Itchy was worried about Fidget. There had to be some way he could communicate with them and save his throat. Then he had an idea.

"When you need to speak to us," Itchy said, "why don't you write it with your claw in the sand? That way we will know when you are hungry or if you need anything."

****

Paw's for Thought

Fidget scowled and made a movement with his paw: he didn't like writing much. Surely there must be another way. He raised his paw to his mouth as if holding something: up and down he raised his paw while looking at Itchy, willing him with his dark eyes to understand what he was trying to explain.

"I know!" Itchy shouted suddenly, smiling at his clever friend. "If you move your paws in a certain way we will understand! You would like a drink! Am I right?"

Fidget grinned at Itchy and nodded vigorously: they had got it! And the water might help his voice to return.

Itchy replied. "We could all do with a drink of water: it's so hot in this country all the time."

So the badgers, still suffering from the effects of the smoke, followed the two mice as closely as they could. It was difficult sometimes and only the tip of Squeaky's tail as she hopped nimbly through the thick undergrowth gave her away.

Two birds sat high in the trees watching the scene below. A hooded robin sat half way up a dead branch next to other birds and chirruped to the plump pigeon who sat beside him with his feathers puffed up.

"Funny looking creatures they are! They must be really hot in their fur coats!"

"Yeah," replied the pigeon, rocking gently against a branch still half-asleep. She half-opened one eye and fanned herself idly with a feathered wing as she said:

"I wonder why they are rushing around."

"Can't see the hurry myself," answered the robin lazily.

Robin and Pigeon discussing the Friends

Soon they came to the waterhole. It was a sight to behold. Itchy had never seen such a beautiful spot. Huge slabs of red rock seemingly balanced quite precariously, one on top of another, overhung the crystal-clear water. Tall, green trees and shrubs had their mirror image reflected softly in the moonlight. Stars twinkled overhead in the night sky, like Upple fairy lights at Christmas, thought Itchy. He sighed wistfully to himself, thinking of his woodland home in winter with his cosy sett and Matty making his favourite worm stew.

Growing nearby were Eucalyptus trees: their leaves moved softly on the night breeze making a soft, shushing sound. They provided much-needed shade for lizards and snakes to hide under from unsuspecting Upple eyes. Cicadas clicked their legs together in unison, making the sound almost deafening to Itchy and his friends. Itchy scratched at his ears as if that would make the sound go away. How much quieter it was back home, he thought, as he wondered again how Matty and the cubs were.

Itchy, Fidget and Norm waded into the cool water, enjoying the feel of it against their fur as it washed away the smoke and dust. They stayed for some time washing, drinking and then grooming themselves on the bank. But Itchy's fur was really troubling him and he scratched and scratched with his sharpest claw to try and get some relief.

Glancing towards the rocks, he noticed in the shade a small branch covered in thorns that would do, he thought. He picked up the stick and began to scratch hard at his back with it.

"Ahh! That's better!" Itchy said out loud to the others in satisfaction as he scratched. The thorns were really getting to the spot; he was having difficulty reaching the centre of his back with his claws and he twisted and turned in an effort to reach the annoying itch. At last! The scratching motion was helping to ease the itching skin beneath his hot fur.

"Ahh!" he said satisfied, grinning with his eyes closed and enjoying the sensation. "There's nothing like a really good scratch!"

"Put! Me! Down! Put! Me! Down!" a very cross voice shouted. Itchy stopped scratching for a moment, surprised: whose voice was that? He turned around to see Norm laughing. Squeaky thought whatever it was, was so funny; she was rolling around in the dusty soil and Fidget was laughing silently and pointing towards Itchy's back.

"What is it?" Itchy asked, puzzled, still holding the thorny twig tightly in his paw.

"Put me down!"came the voice again, getting even more irritated. Itchy looked at the stick: it had started to wriggle frantically around! It had a face! And it was speaking crossly to him! A stick with a face!

Itchy bent down and carefully placed the strange creature back onto the big rock where he had found him.

"Oh! I'm sorry! I thought you were a stick with thorns on! What on Badger's earth are you?" He bent down to look closer, surprise etched across his badger's brow in amazement.

Itchy scratches his back with the stick

"I," the lizard announced proudly, stretching his neck with its bark-like skin upwards as he spoke, annoyed that he was unknown to this strange creature in thick fur and had been treated in such a way.

"I am a Thorny lizard!" The reptile shook his body indignantly, shaking his thorns back into their correct place.

"And I look nothing like a stick!" With that, the lizard stomped over to the shade under the leaves, muttering under his breath about the fact he was lucky not to have lost any of his thorns. There he was relaxing in the shadows when he was suddenly picked up by a stranger and used as a scratching stick! The cheek of it!

The friends settled down to eat worms and any witchetty grubs they could find, teasing Itchy good-naturedly about his mistaken identity of the lizard. Norm didn't really want grubs again; he fancied pizza but he didn't like to complain and so far he hadn't found any lying around, not even a half-eaten piece of cheese crust or a soggy tomato.

****

A Sticky Cure

"Cough, cough," Fidget went quietly, as he tried in vain to clear his throat, which was still sore.

"What can we do to help Fidget now?" Itchy asked Norm and Squeaky between chewing on mouthfuls of fat, juicy grubs, which weren't too bad once you got used to them. Norm suggested he gargle with some of the water, but Fidget had already tried that and it hadn't worked.

"There is something else we could try," Squeaky said in her high voice, her long whiskers twitching madly from side to side, as she hopped, skipped and jumped into the air again and again.

"Some Eucalyptus trees have a red sap which can be used to cure things; it's called a Bloodwood tree, because its sap is dark red. Fidget could try that."

"Look," she said pointing to a group of trees, "there's one over there."

With that she tumbled over and scurried round in circles, pleased that she had been able to help her new friends.

Fidget wasn't keen and pulled an unhappy face at this suggestion, waving his paws to say he would almost rather not speak than try and eat a tree.

He was fussy with the worms that he ate and really didn't fancy some red stuff from a tree: it might taste horrid. However, if he could get his voice and whistle back, maybe anything was worth a try, even if it did taste disgusting! Fidget decided it might be worth a try especially if it pleased his friends, he could see they were trying to help.

So he wandered over to the area Squeaky pointed to, reluctantly encouraged by Itchy and Norm. It was alright for them; he thought grumpily: it wasn't them who had to eat this stuff. He put his claws against the side of one of the trees which looked as if it was dying. The bark was peeling off it in thick chunks, but bravely Fidget closed his eyes and with his friend's encouragements ringing in his ears, he cautiously stuck his tongue out and gingerly licked at the red sap seeping from the tree.

"Ugh! Ugh! Are you sure this will help?" Fidget whispered, eyes screwed up tightly closed as he tasted it.

Then, "cough, cough" and, "cough" again, but at least the others could hear him a bit better, even if he wasn't very loud! His voice was rough as he complained constantly about the taste; he stuck his tongue out in disgust, showing the others the sticky goo which clung to the sides of his mouth and his nose.

Itchy encouraged Fidget not to give up; after all, he had only had a couple of mouthfuls.

"Keep trying," he said. "It will take more than one lick! You can't give up!"

Norm, feeling sorry for his friend as he didn't fancy the red goo either, carried over some ants for him to mix into the foul-tasting stuff.

"Here try this," he said, offering a pile of crawling ants to the reluctant badger. "It might make it taste a little better."

Not wanting to appear ungrateful, Fidget reluctantly put some of the ants on his tongue and then licked quickly at the red sap, gulping down as much as he could before the ants could tickle. At least the sticky liquid seemed to coat his sore throat and ease the pain.

Fidget with ants on his tongue

A few spluttering coughs later and Fidget could whisper enough to be heard!

"Hurrah!" he said in a low voice. "Can you hear me?" Cough. "I'm almost cured!" He smiled, as he knew he still wasn't speaking very loudly, but a whisper was better than no sound at all, and the soreness in his throat had eased.

Itchy and Norm looked at each other relieved for Fidget.

"It will be a while before he can speak properly," said Squeaky, "Fidget needs to rest it really."

"I know," Itchy replied, "but at least we can understand him through his paw language. We just have to be facing him if he wants to ask us something."

Fidget interrupted them, confident it was only a matter of time. He whispered:

"Now all I need to do is practise. I can't wait to get home to see Hurryup; she will be wondering where I am all this time!

I can't wait to tell everyone back home about our adventure."

The talk of Badger Wood and Hurryup reminded Itchy again of Matty and the family and friends he had left behind. So although he was glad Fidget seemed to be recovering, he was feeling a little sad: after all they were still lost and miles from home.

"Come on," he said scratching his thigh roughly as he turned his back to them and walked away, trying to stop the tears, which had unexpectedly sprung into his eyes. Pretending to have dust in them, he rubbed roughly at his face. Itchy didn't want to seem down and felt he must be strong for the others.

Itchy swallowed hard to clear the lump in his throat as he said gruffly:

"Come on, it's no good sitting here. We must be on our way to Uluru to see if it holds the route home we have been looking for.

Travelling during the starlit night when there were less Upples around, they followed Squeaky, but it took a long time, because if she wasn't looking for crumbs the Upples may have left, she was doing somersaults. The two badgers and Norm survived on witchetty grubs, snails and soft grass. Uluru still seemed quite a distance away.

****

Dinosaur Bones

At dawn they huddled together near a small group of shrubs which provided some shade, but the friends could not get comfortable. The earth was dry, hard and cracked in places due to lack of rain, but they were used to that by now. Whichever way they sat, something was digging into them. What was it that seemed to be lying just under the soil's surface? The two badgers scratched hard at the sandy dirt, digging to see exactly what was stopping them from settling down; it was a very, very, large, white bone.

"I don't know what this is," announced Itchy, trying to get his claws under the shape enough to lift it out of the way. He was fed up with trying to get to sleep. "But, ouch! I nearly broke a claw: whatever it is, it's huge! And it's heavy."

"Me too," Fidget whispered with his paw, pointing to himself and frowning. He wriggled about at the best of times, but it was impossible to sleep on this lumpy, rock-hard surface.

"And me," said Norm forlornly, his eyes half-closed. He had just been dozing off, had started dreaming about pizza and wasn't happy at being disturbed. Walking during the darkness he was tired and needed his sleep during the Upple daylight hours.

"I think I know what it is!" Squeaky said excitedly. "And we can't move it!"

"Why not?" Itchy replied, thinking he could dig under it and move it away.

"It's too big!" Squeaky squealed excitedly, leaping high into the air.

"It's been in the ground too long! We will have to find somewhere else to rest: the Upples will be all around us if they discover what's here! It's a dinosaur bone! They were huge creatures that roamed all over the earth."

Itchy scratched at his side in bewilderment; he had never heard of such creatures and there were certainly none at home in Badger Wood.

Squeaky could barely contain herself, the excitement sounding in her voice; she loved to tell the friends things about her home and the Outback in Australia.

"Not many have been found in Australia. The bone you are sitting on must be at least one and a half Upple metres long! I grew up hearing how my ancestors used to run away from them. They would call out and warn each other if they saw one coming! I think it could be called a **Doyouthinkhesawus**: that's what one of my ancestors used to shout, and they lived here millions of years ago, they were huge! Bigger even than an Upple bus! Lots of Upples arrive looking for them, and then they take ages to dig them up! And then!"

The Friends find a Dinosaur Bone

Squeaky took a breath and paused for effect; she enjoyed seeing the horrified look on the friends' faces as they gathered around her.

"They put them in a place called a museum for other Upples to come and look at them!"

"Funny creatures, Upples," Norm said, flicking bits of dry mud from his coat and stepping away from the bone. Fidget nodded in agreement, wrinkled his brow and whispered to Itchy:

"Why on Badger's earth would anyone want to look at old bones?"

The friends got up quickly, looking around them to make sure no Upples were nearby. It was no good: they would have to find somewhere else to sleep. None of the friends could feel comfortable sleeping here now. With the sun getting hotter, they had to find shade quickly. Itchy and Fidget felt as if they were dragging themselves around. Finally they found some shade near rocks and they dozed on and off until nightfall.

Later that night the friends sat eating witchetty grubs and discussing what to do next. Fidget made some signs with his paw to tell Norm and Itchy that the route near the dinosaur bones was out of the question: it was too dangerous and Upples might be nearby. It was lucky that Squeaky knew her way around this area.

****

The Colourful Rock

The three friends followed Squeaky through some dense, scrubby undergrowth and then across the red earth for several hours until they saw a magnificent sight. A huge rock, a mound, seemed to rise up out of the earth's flat surface. Bathed in the early morning light of a wondrous dawn sky, Uluru seemed almost magical. It seemed to emit a soft, orangey glow. Itchy, Fidget and Norm gazed at it in wonder: they had never seen such a beautiful sight.

"Did you know?" Squeaky said, smiling, her whiskers once more twitching wildly, picking up the sounds and smells of the desert.

"That most of Uluru is hidden underground, so maybe there are some tunnels for you to follow and find your way back home!" She hopped up in the air and did a backward flip with excitement at this thought.

"Underground! Did you say?" Itchy was astonished! He thought maybe he had heard Squeaky wrong.

"Underground!" he repeated, looking first at Norm then at Fidget to see if they had heard as well.

"Indigenous people call it Uluru but it is also called Ayers Rock by other Upples," announced Squeaky, thrilled she could inform Itchy, Fidget and Norm where they were and tell them all about it.

"It is estimated that it is around six hundred million years old and it would originally have been at the bottom of the sea. Some two and a half Upples kilometres of it are underneath the ground, isn't that amazing? Let's go closer and we can have a look round before too many tourists arrive: Upples love to see it in this light."

Already they could see coaches arriving with travellers all eager to get a glimpse of the famous landmark and sacred place of the indigenous people. So the friends crept round to the back of the rock, which was quite a walk, where they were hidden from Upple view.

Huge openings had been made in the side of Uluru: Upple or nature-made? Itchy wasn't sure, but it was certainly a magnificent sight! Such wonderful brightly coloured paintings, of wild animals, lizards and birds dominated the walls of the caves. In one place it looked as if Upple hands had been dipped in yellow paint and then pressed in patterns on the cave walls nearby, which seemed to Itchy to be badgers' years old.

Cave paintings in Uluru

"I wonder why they did these?" thought Itchy out loud as he gazed around in wonder, using his claw to trace the old Aboriginal images.

Then he asked, "Do you think this is the way home, Squeaky? Can we get back to Badger Wood from here?"

"I don't know...", Squeaky replied uncertainly. Her whiskers were twitching wildly: she had never heard of anyone going anywhere from tunnels in Uluru. All the animals she knew lived in Australia all the time. Why would they want to leave Australia anyway? It was the perfect place for a mouse.

"Shh!" Fidget motioned quietly, putting a claw to his lips. He pointed to his ear as if to say, "I can hear Upples! And they are not far away!"

"It's nearly our night-time anyway," Itchy whispered to his friend, looking round.

"We ought to get some rest: it will be a big day tomorrow and we will see if we can travel down through Uluru and find our way back to Badger Wood."

Sure enough, sitting in a small group, chatting and eating, the Upples were totally unaware of the friends huddled together watching them warily. Itchy, Fidget and Norm sniffed the air that had that odd, distinct smelly smell of Upples. It lingered and Itchy, wrinkling his nose in distaste, knew it could be smelt by all animals quite a distance away.

Squeaky then showed Itchy, Fidget and Norm into a small cave, which had an opening on a side away from the visitors, and they crept in. They slept soundly all day, while sightseers oblivious to the animals nearby, gazed in wonder at the amazing landscape.

At dusk, Itchy stood up on his hind legs, just as he used to do at home in Badger Wood, stretched and opened his mouth in a wide yawn. The sunset of blue and orange stripes lighting up the sky looked stunning. They watched, as the last dying rays of the hot sun disappeared over the horizon.

"Come on!" Itchy urged his friends excitedly. He scratched at his thigh as he got to his feet, keen to be on his way.

"Now Fidget's voice is a little better we can go home!"

The three friends only had to decide which one of the caves to follow.

"How on Badger's earth will we choose?" whispered Fidget, smiling from ear to ear. He was feeling happy; he had been practising with his paw signing on and off for hours now and his friends could understand everything! And they were on their way home, he was convinced of it.

"Surely," answered Squeaky, jumping into the air, "it would be the biggest cave that would lead you the right way."

"Not necessarily," answered Itchy frowning and scratching his brow.

"We followed Auntie Twiddle's map down a very old tunnel before and that wasn't very big. We had to crawl almost flat in places. We made a mistake, though: we were supposed to travel during badger's day when the Upples were asleep, but because it was dark due to a solar eclipse, we journeyed at the wrong time and ended up here, in Australia, instead of a new woodland home!"

The droning of a small aircraft carrying Upples as it flew overhead disturbed them, just as they were thinking of getting some juicy grubs for supper.

"Quick!" Itchy called out to his friends. "Hide! We will be seen by the Upples in the plane!"

As the Upples chatted to one another about the glorious colour of Uluru and the magnificent sky, Itchy, Fidget and Norm bent low and rushed to hide from their view. They couldn't afford to be captured now, not when they were so close to going home. Quickly saying goodbye to Squeaky as she disappeared into long grass, they ran into the nearest cave. Although it wasn't as big as some of the others, the opening seemed to dip downwards slightly, as they made their way along the narrowing sandy path.

"This could well be our way home to Badger Wood," announced Itchy gleefully as he glanced over his shoulder to Fidget and Norm who were following closely behind him.

"Oh I do hope so!" Norm laughed in reply, the thought of his favourite cheese and tomato pizza not far from his mind. He patted his belly as it rumbled noisily in anticipation.

The reddish tunnel twisted and turned along a path as the trio cautiously made their way. The hope was that before long they would see daylight and the familiar shapes of green trees that meant they were nearly home.

They walked downwards for several Upple days; happy to be on their way at last, but with the grubs now running out, the friends were becoming increasingly hungry. Itchy didn't recall their journey taking so long when they left home, and hoped they were going in the right direction. At the end of the path which had begun to rise upwards sharply, their hearts sank. The tunnel appeared to be blocked by a gigantic boulder. It was at least two Upples high and one Upple width across: how on Badger's earth would they get past that? Itchy thought sadly his mood taking a downturn.

A large boulder blocks the way out

"Maybe we can move it if we all try together," Norm said, almost as if he could read what Itchy was thinking. So, with a huge effort the three friends leant against the boulder and pushed hard, but it was no good. Although it had been eroded until its surface was smooth, it refused to move no matter how hard they tried. Just at the edge they could see a glimmer of daylight which gave Itchy an idea.

He raised his brow, scratched hard at his leg, and said, "We could tunnel under it, it's quite soft sand underneath: if we use our claws we might just be able to dig out enough to squeeze through the space to get to the other side. What do you think?"

Norm shrugged his shoulders and looked at Fidget. He didn't really want to go back the way they had come: it was quite a distance and he had been looking forward to having some pizza.

"We haven't lost anything by trying," he said, sighing, and resigning himself to the fact pizza was nowhere near.

"If you and Fidget dig, I can use my paws and tail to scoop the sand out of the way; we can do it if we all work together. It's either that or we turn back and choose a different route."

The three friends were by now very hungry, so they decided to try and dig away a space. They dug and dug furiously until a small, badger-sized hole was made under the bottom edge of the huge, red lump which stood in their way. The wind whistled through the gap, bringing desert sand and buzzing flies into the tunnel and covering their fur in gritty debris.

Itchy bent down to look through to the other side and had to put a paw over his eyes, as he, too, was showered with even more red sand, which made him itch once more. Fidget and Norm turned their backs to the wind which howled in, bringing with it even more sand and clouds, upon clouds of black flies. Should they face this raging wind and risk what lay on the other side?

They took a deep breath and with the thought of Badger Wood awaiting them, the three friends held paws tightly and wriggled one by one through the narrow gap they had made. It was a tight fit but they could just about squeeze through.

When, WHOOSH! All three were sucked upwards, together, clean out of the tunnel and up, up into the air!

Over and over they were tossed about. Unable to hold onto each other any longer, the badgers and the very big mouse tumbled separately through the wind. Round and round in circles as they were swept high above the ground and up into a grey, very forbidding, stormy-looking sky. Up, almost to the top of the clouds into a cone shape of a grey wooliness, the animals were helpless.

The three friends get Blown Away!

As Itchy looked around him he could see Fidget and Norm were also being turned upside down and bits of Upples belongings began swirling in front of his eyes. Bits of house roofs, and Upple cars spun, seemingly picked up at odd moments and dropped at random before other bits and pieces took their place. I must be dreaming thought Itchy as pieces of clothes, trees and other animals drifted past his tired eyes just before he fell in to a deep sleep. He had no idea how long they were all in the air for, when.

THUD, THUD, THUD! They landed one after the other a few Upples' height apart. It took a few moments for Itchy to come to his senses and have a look around him. Brushing his tatty, windswept fur down and making sure he was still in one piece, he gave himself a good scratch as he looked around for his friends and wondered where on Badger's earth they could be?

This earth didn't look red like the Australian earth. The ground was now a greyish colour.

Fidget stood up, brushing the dirt briskly from his black and white coat, while giving out a soft whisper in approval of his surroundings. They were somewhere completely different. Maybe we are home, he thought, coughing gently and trying not to strain his throat.

"I don't know where we are," said Norm taking in the view whilst checking his arms, legs and tail were all still there. It was night-time but the sky was clear and it was still fairly warm. Then, Fidget spotted something and pointed into the distance waving his paws excitedly at the others and jumping up and down with joy.

"That sign, look! That sign! What does it say?" He couldn't help but let out a shout in his excitement, pointing urgently at large, white letters on the hilltop in front of them as he jumped up and down.

He spelled out H O L L Y W O O D in big white letters. Itchy put his arms up in triumph!

*Itchy, arms outstretched near the
Hollywood sign*

"HOLLYWOOD! It says Hollywood! We _must_ be nearly home, then!" he announced, looking at the others with a big smile on his badger's face.

"We must be near Badger Wood, don't you think so?" Itchy said still grinning from ear to ear, as he looked first at Fidget, then towards Norm who was sniffing the night air hoping for his favourite smell of pizza, cooking softly with cheese and tomato on top.

"Maybe..." replied Norm cautiously. He was not convinced and he couldn't smell pizza either. He couldn't see any sign of spring flowers or the familiar tree shapes of the English countryside. But the sign did say Hollywood: maybe it was a wood comprised of holly trees? Itchy was right, maybe they were near Badger Wood at last: the name on the sign even sounded similar.

"If we go closer to the sign and have a good look around, nearer or over the top of that hill, we might find our wood we are looking for!" Itchy declared happily.

Marching forward quickly, he started to make his way up a slight incline, waving happily for his friends to join him.

"You won't find any woods over there," called out a soft, purring voice, causing Itchy to stop in his tracks. He looked over his shoulder towards his friends.

Norm stood still. He thought the voice sounded American: he had overheard a film with a voice like this when he was near Samuel's house. Surely they couldn't be in America! Could they? How could this be possible?

There didn't seem to be anyone nearby, but as they looked closer they could see a large cat peering at them through the darkness; the friends hadn't noticed him, as the colour of his coat blended in to the surroundings so well it had made him nearly invisible. Only his piercing green eyes gave away his position. Then he moved and through the darkness they could see his ears were turned down against the slightly scruffy, beige fur on the top of his head.

"My name..." announced the cat nonchalantly, as he casually strolled over towards them, large paws padding softly on the earth.

"Is P-22, I'm a mountain lion, just one of the many animals that live here." The lion grinned. "There are owls, deer and coyotes, too. But it's the Upples you need to be afraid of," he said smiling broadly as he sensed the animals' fear.

Despite these assurances, Norm quivered: he wasn't sure if the lion was friendly or not; he might just fancy a large mouse for his supper! He moved away to stand slightly behind Itchy and Fidget. They, too, were feeling uneasy as the lion ran a rough tongue around his yellowing teeth and licked at the corner of his mouth, which had a small amount of dribble starting to form. The lion was so close to them they could almost feel his warm breath; it didn't smell very pleasant either.

Itchy could sense his fur standing on end down the length of his backbone and he gave an involuntary shiver as he met Fidget's worried glance.

"What kind of name is that for an animal?" Itchy asked, cautiously trying not to show how uneasy he was in the lion's company.

"Surely an Upple must have given you that name? What's your real name, the one your mother gave you?"

"It's Roamin," purred the cat, grinning at them as he stood just a short distance away, his eyes sparkling in the darkness. "I was ill some time ago: seems I had drunk some water which was poisonous, but an Upple found me and made me better. They are not all bad. There is a lake near here, Hollywood Lake; you might like a drink of water, as it may help you recover after your long journey. I couldn't help overhearing your conversation and you may be right, perhaps you are near the end and you have reached your final destination." He trailed off, leaving Norm even more uncomfortable.

Roamin (American Mountain Lion)

Norm was not the only one who didn't feel comfortable in the lions company. They were all becoming increasingly uneasy the more the lion spoke and he seemed very sure of himself.

"Come on guys follow me," Roamin said persuasively, rubbing a paw across his bent and somewhat chewed ear. His large paws padded softly on the ground as he walked away. There was a distinct keenness in his throaty growl, as he turned and started to stroll up the hill towards more dense undergrowth.

"We need to travel at night though, for during the day Hollywood gets very busy with Upples." He smiled at them, and while purring reassuringly he was convinced these new animals would follow him.

He had once caused quite a stir when he had been out during the day: Upples had filmed his every move. If he stayed near the park area which covered some four thousand Upple acres, he was rarely seen. Anyway, Roamin didn't really want to be the centre of attention again, especially as he now had supper on his agenda. He licked his lips in anticipation of his meal. Enticing the friends all the time while keeping up his soft conversation, he glanced casually at them now and then over his shoulder as he strolled ahead, as if he didn't care whether they were following him or not.

"Do you think he can really help us get home?" Norm whispered in Itchy's ear, his knees knocking together, to which Itchy replied:

"No, I think he may mean to eat us for his supper! We need to keep our distance from him!"

Then Itchy heard a sound, almost like a dog barking.

"Bark! Bark!"

****

Groundhog Day

It sounded like an Upple dog but there was no one to be seen. Then, another noise, almost as if someone was grinding his teeth between barks! The noise was amazing! The area acted almost like an amphitheatre: the sound surrounded them, seemingly coming from all directions.

"Over here! Psst! Psst!" Then, the grinding noise again. "Quickly or he will see you!"

Half-hidden underneath a prickly bush was a furry head sticking out of a burrow. He had a greyish tinge to the top of its coat, which looked as if it had been touched by frost, but was reddish underneath.

Then, to their surprise out popped a creature that looked like a big, fat squirrel. He had long, curved claws and huge front teeth. It was a groundhog. He stood up to his full height, which was about up to Itchy and Fidget's shoulders, beckoning wildly with his paw for the friends to come over. He looked frantically from left to right for danger. Putting his claws to his mouth he let out an almighty whistle; his tail stood up on end like a stiff brush as he waved his paw at the friends more urgently.

Itchy, Fidget and Norm didn't need to be asked twice! They ran over as quickly as they could to the groundhog's burrow, but oh no! They couldn't quite fit in! The burrow was slightly too narrow so Itchy and Fidget began to dig furiously, hoping to get into the underground burrow before the mountain lion could see where they had disappeared to.

Luckily the lion still had his back to them as he was trying not to cause them alarm. The strange sounds of the groundhogs barking and whistling to each other filled the cool evening air.

All around them heads began to pop up from different entrances, all the time distracting the lion's attention with these odd noises; he didn't know where to look.

Once inside, the biggest, strongest groundhog put a hind paw against the side of the burrow and pulled the friends by the paws inside. One by one and with a pop, they tumbled head first into the tunnel and safety.

Just in time! The three friends had managed to disappear from view and so the lion ambled slowly away, wondering to himself where his supper had vanished to: these groundhogs were a nuisance. Shame, he hadn't eaten in a while and that big mouse had looked mighty tasty, he thought to himself, idly sighing.

"My name," pant, pant, went the groundhog's breath in short, sharp gasps.

"Is Repeater," he said, whistling through his teeth as he leant against the dirt wall recovering from the exertion. He wondered aloud what these animals were.

Repeater the groundhog

Itchy scratched at his coat and Fidget gave out a sigh of relief while poor Norm was still trembling.

The only black and white creatures the groundhogs had seen recently were skunks or raccoons, and these new friends weren't either of those. No black mask over the eyes, like a racoon, and no strong smell of the skunk either. What were they doing here? Maybe the storm had something to do with it? All sorts of strange things could happen when the weather played up.

Repeater looked at Itchy trying to find an explanation and said:

"Only yesterday there was a really bumpy looking sky filled with what Upples call mammatus or bubble clouds. They are caused by a change in the air temperature or moisture. Massive quantities of water vapour make this happen before a thunderstorm, or a tornado. They take the appearance of hundreds of little balls with round pouches caused by the sinking air. Although with the light on them they looked wonderful, all the animals know they need to shelter until the strong wind that was coming had passed by."

He stroked his whiskers with a long claw before continuing, his voice steadier now.

"We knew something odd was about to happen and now...," he said with a sharp intake of breath and shaking his head in amazement at Itchy, "you and your friends have arrived."

Itchy explained how they had got caught up in a vast storm when they were trying to leave Uluru and had somehow landed near this place called Hollywood.

"We are trying to get home to Badger Wood and our family and friends," replied Itchy, scratching at his thigh, relieved to be out of the lion's way. He told them all about the Upples and how they wanted to build on their woodland home.

The groundhogs were fascinated and vowed to do all they could to help the friends to return home. Repeater told them how groundhogs had once saved their home by digging and uncovering an archaeological site, so they knew all about the dangers caused by Upples.

"This is my cousin, Ditto," said Repeater, Ditto nodded and moved in exactly the same way as Repeater.

"And this", he said pointing to an older, greying groundhog with glasses, sitting in the centre of a big room, "is Chuck. He knows all about travel: he's always deep in concentration when he's reading."

On hearing his name mentioned, Chuck looked up, wrinkled his nose and peered over the top of a map book he was studying. He squinted at the friends. He was used to saving all manner of creatures but these were certainly strangers around these parts. Chuck looked at Repeater concerned: they were busy doing the same thing day after day anyway and he wasn't sure how they could help, despite Repeaters assurances.

"All our family live and work together. Come with me and I will show you around and tell you what we do. We, too, are plagued by Upples, as well as the mountain lion that nearly ate you. It's a dangerous world out there. Our job is to protect other animals from these threats, so we have a network of tunnels with   teams, who take it in turns to act as look out."

The groundhog opened his paws as wide as they would go to illustrate the size of the area they covered.

He continued. "We communicate with each other with bark-like noises so the Upples think it could be one of their dogs. We also grind our teeth in warning or whistle to one another. It's all like a code you see: only animals can understand it."

Repeater showed Itchy and his friends round the headquarters they had created. Several large rooms led off a main entrance with yet more corridors. It was a real hive of activity as groundhogs of all shapes, sizes and ages were all busy protecting the area around Hollywood. Taking it in turns to pop up and down at regular intervals they were certainly keeping watch.

"Got to go! Got to go! Go! Go! Go!" shouted Repeater suddenly, making his way quickly to the entrance, as the sound of groundhogs barking and various whistles sounded loudly through the tunnels.

Then, a small, furry creature came hurtling through the entrance and landed in a heap on the floor. It was Wanda!

Wanda lands in a heap on the floor

"What are you doing here?!" asked Itchy, wide-eyed in amazement. He couldn't believe it! Wanda hadn't been near them when they had made their way into Uluru. How on Badger's earth had she got here?

If Wanda was here, how on Badger's earth had that happened?

And how were they ever going to leave the safety of the groundhogs to get home and avoid the Mountain Lion who lay in wait for them?

Will the friends get back in time to save Badger Wood or are they destined to be travelling, forever searching for a new home?

Itchy's journey continues in Book 7